The
STORM DRAGON

MORE MAGICAL RESCUES!

The Sky Unicorn

COMING SOON:

The Baby Firebird
The Magic Fox

The
STORM DRAGON

By Paula Harrison

Illustrated by SOPHY WILLIAMS

ALADDIN

New York   London   Toronto   Sydney   New Delhi

ALADDIN

An imprint of Simon & Schuster Children's Publishing Division

1230 Avenue of the Americas, New York, New York 10020

First Aladdin paperback edition March 2017

Text copyright © 2015 by Paula Harrison

Illustrations copyright © 2015 by Sophy Williams

Originally published in the United Kingdom in 2015 by Nosy Crow Ltd

Published by arrangement with Nosy Crow

Also available in an Aladdin hardcover edition.

All rights reserved, including the right of reproduction in whole or in part in any form.

ALADDIN and related logo are registered trademarks of Simon & Schuster, Inc.

For information about special discounts for bulk purchases, please contact Simon & Schuster Special Sales at 1-866-506-1949 or business@simonandschuster.com.

The Simon & Schuster Speakers Bureau can bring authors to your live event.

For more information or to book an event contact the Simon & Schuster Speakers Bureau at 1-866-248-3049 or visit our website at www.simonspeakers.com.

Cover designed by Karina Granda

Interior designed by Tom Daly

The text of this book was set in ITC Clearface.

Manufactured in the United States of America 1118 OFF

4 6 8 10 9 7 5

Library of Congress Control Number: 2016932246

ISBN 978-1-4814-7608-9 (hc)

ISBN 978-1-4814-7607-2 (pbk)

ISBN 978-1-4814-7609-6 (eBook)

The
STORM DRAGON

Chapter One

★ ⋅ ⁖ ✳

The Golden Songbird

Sophy hurried out of the castle door carrying a heavy wooden chair. She stopped at the bottom of the steps to get her breath back. Her arms ached from lifting things all morning!

A gentle breeze blew across the castle battlements, ruffling her wavy golden hair.

"Hurry up, Sophy! There's no time to dawdle." Mrs. Ricker marched down the steps, her eyes bulging behind her spectacles. "And tie your hair back at once. I don't want the queen to see you looking so messy."

Mrs. Ricker was the royal housekeeper. She was the kind of person who could spot untidy hair or a dirty apron from miles away!

"Yes, Mrs. Ricker." Sophy searched her apron pocket for a hair bobble and quickly braided her hair. Her parents had died when she was little, and she'd worked as a maid at Greytowers Castle ever since. She was used to the housekeeper's strict ways.

Mrs. Ricker went back inside. Sophy picked up the chair again and walked across the wooden drawbridge. The castle was circled by a moat filled with water, and the drawbridge was the only way to get across.

When she reached the other side, Sophy set down the chair and gazed around. Greytowers Castle stood on a hill, and the view from the top was amazing.

The Kingdom of Arramia stretched out in every direction, with its thick forests, bright rivers, and majestic, snowy mountains. Two planets hung together in the sky, a green one and a smaller purple one.

Sophy loved the story of how the planets grew by magic in the air. Storytellers visiting the castle would often tell the tale, and she would hide behind the door to listen. Sometimes the storytellers would talk of magical animals such as unicorns, star wolves, cloud bears, and dragons. Then Sophy would promise herself that one day she'd leave the castle to go to look for the creatures in those stories!

She shaded her eyes to peer into the distance.

Beyond the fields was a huge forest that stretched for miles. Away to the west a silver river wound along the valley. Sophy had heard of many magical animals, but she'd never seen any of them. Could there be a star wolf in that forest . . . or a unicorn by that river? She was too far away to see, and it wasn't likely the creatures would ever come closer to the castle.

Not everyone was kind to magical animals, but Sophy didn't really know why. The queen's favorite knight, Sir Fitzroy, had once declared he thought it was wrong for creatures to have magical powers at all.

Sighing, Sophy dragged the chair round the corner to the gatehouse. The ground was covered with tables, chairs, wardrobes, and boxes. Queen Viola had decided to get rid of some palace furniture, along with the old king's belongings. King Rupert had died the year before. He'd been a great collector, so there were an awful lot of things the queen wanted to throw away!

A boy with a freckled face leaped out from behind a wardrobe. "Hey, Sophy!"

"Tom!" Sophy gasped. "Don't make me jump like that!"

"Sorry!" Tom grinned and wiped his hands on his muddy trousers. "Is there much more to fetch?"

"No, that's it."

"Good. I don't think I'd be able to fit anything else on the cart." Tom went off, whistling.

Sophy walked around the mountain of stuff. The old furniture was going to Ingleton, a nearby village, to be sold at the market. Tom, who worked in the gardens, would be taking it there in the cart. Among the worn-out chairs and tables Sophy could see the old king's belongings. There was a pile of rolled-up maps, a huge telescope, and towers of old books with titles such as *Paths Across the Heskia Mountains*. It made Sophy feel sad seeing the unwanted books piled up on the ground.

Then she noticed something else and gasped.

On the grass, under a table, was a small black chest with a silver lock. Sophy recognized it straightaway. The king had collected crystals and kept them in that chest. She'd only seen them once, when the king had opened the box as she was passing by. She'd never forgotten the dazzling beauty of the stones inside. Surely the queen hadn't thrown *them* away?

Her heart thumping, she climbed over two chairs and scrambled under the table to get to the chest. Her apron was really grubby now, but she didn't care. Her fingers struggled with the silver catch, but eventually she opened it and pulled up the lid. Crystals of every color, from ruby red to emerald green and sapphire blue, gleamed inside the box. Sophy took out a deep-blue one and held it in the palm of her hand.

This was the color she'd always imagined the sea might be.

A fluttering noise made her look up. A golden songbird flew down and perched on the back of a chair, watching her with beady black eyes. Sophy put the blue crystal back, suddenly feeling as if she was doing something wrong.

The bird fluffed up its golden feathers and let out a trill of beautiful music.

Sophy had never heard anything so lovely.

She hoped the bird might sing again, but instead it fluttered down beside her. Then it hopped onto the edge of the chest and tilted its head, eyeing first Sophy and then the crystals.

"They're beautiful, aren't they?" said Sophy.

The songbird hopped right into the middle of the crystals and flapped its wings, scattering stones out of the chest and onto the ground.

"Stop!" cried Sophy, trying to catch the spilling crystals. "We'll lose them if you do that."

But the songbird went on beating its wings, sending more stones flying. At last it stopped and pecked at the remaining crystals. Sophy leaned closer. It was trying to get at something beneath the stones. The bird had a piece of purple material in its beak, and it pulled and pulled. Finally the bird let go of the cloth and gave an impatient trill. It was almost as though it was asking her to help.

"What have you found?" Sophy took hold of the purple material and pulled it free of the crystals. She found herself holding a small cloth bag that had something heavy inside. The songbird fluffed its feathers again a. expectantly.

Sophy's fingers tingled as she undid the dra. string bag and reached in. Her hand brushed against rough stone. The purse was full of small pieces of rock. She took one out and studied its lumpy, gray surface.

The bird gave a final burst of song; then, without another look at the bag or at Sophy, it flew off.

Sophy frowned at the rough stone. All that fuss about bumpy pieces of rock? She'd thought the songbird was trying to show her something . . . but why this?

A swirl of wind lifted her hair, and a shaft of light beamed down on the stone's rough edges. Sophy felt a strange tumbling in her stomach as if something was about to happen.

"Sophy!" Mrs. Ricker's footsteps pounded on the drawbridge.

Sophy quickly crawled out from under the table. She'd lost track of the time! She dropped the little stone into the bag and put the bag in her apron pocket. Then she scooped the crystals back into the chest and climbed over the furniture.

"Coming, Mrs. Ricker!" she called, rushing off toward the castle.

Chapter Two

★ ⋅∗⋅ ★

Crash Landing

Sophy was so busy after that that she didn't have time to think about the golden songbird or look inside the little purple bag in her apron pocket.

She swept the floor in the throne room, polished all of the queen's crowns, and helped Cook decorate a huge chocolate cake that would be served to Her Majesty at teatime.

After that Sophy went to gather apples in the orchard. She worked quickly, picking all the ripe fruit on the lower branches and then fetching a ladder to reach the apples higher up.

She'd just filled a second basket when she heard shouting on the other side of the garden. The wind suddenly blew strongly, making the apple trees sway. Sophy's ladder rocked too, and she held on tight to keep her balance.

A purple shape zoomed overhead, and a terrible screech sent a shiver down her back. The awful cry ended in a thump, followed by the sound of cracking branches. Something had hit one of the apple trees!

Sophy quickly climbed down the ladder and hurried through the orchard. Broken branches lay on the ground not far away, and leaves were floating down. Setting down her basket, she went closer. Had a bird crashed into the tree? It must have been a pretty big one to cause so much damage—maybe a raven or an eagle.

The poor thing could be badly hurt.

As she got nearer, she saw that half of the tree's branches were snapped off and there was a long black mark across its trunk. Something wriggled under one of the broken branches, and a puff of gray dust drifted into the air.

Sophy spun round to call for help, but a whimpering noise stopped her. That didn't sound like a bird! Her heart began to race. Maybe that puff of gray wasn't dust at all. Maybe it was smoke. An amazing thought popped into her

head as she crept right up to the damaged tree.

Hardly daring to breathe, she crouched down and lifted up the broken branch. The creature hiding underneath was purple. Its skin looked soft, but it had bumpy ridges running down its back and along its tail. Another puff of smoke rose from its nostrils as it coughed. Then it rolled over onto four clawed feet, shook its weblike wings, and looked at Sophy with wide, amber eyes.

Sophy knew what it was. She'd listened carefully to many tales about these magical creatures.

This was a dragon.

"Are you real?" Sophy whispered, reaching out to touch the creature.

The dragon gave a snort of alarm and jumped backward. Its amber eyes narrowed, fixing on Sophy. A gust of wind rustled the leaves on the trees.

"It's all right! I won't hurt you," Sophy said gently. The creature was smaller than she'd thought a dragon would be—a little shorter than the gardener's dog. The roundness of its cute purple snout made it look a bit like a puppy.

The dragon crept toward her and sniffed her hand, swishing its long purple tail.

"That's it. . . . I won't hurt you," Sophy repeated.

The dragon came even closer, till she could feel its warm breath on her face. Then it gave her cheek a long, slobbery lick and sat back on its haunches.

Sophy laughed and tried to wipe off the slobber. She glanced at the broken apple tree. "I guess you didn't mean to land here. I wonder why you crashed."

The little dragon sniffed the air and then tried to stretch out its webbed wings, but its left one wouldn't straighten. The dragon tried again, but the left wing dangled uselessly by its side. At last the dragon gave up, and a large tear rolled out of its eye and dripped onto the ground.

"You poor thing—you're injured!" cried Sophy. "Does it really hurt?"

The little dragon sank to the ground, still crying. Sophy patted its bumpy back, wishing she knew what to do. The creature's sobbing was mixed with a dragonish growling, as if it were trying to talk to her. The wind rose again, bending the trees and sending leaves skittering along the ground.

"Oh dear! I wish I knew how to help you," said Sophy. "It must have been horrible crashing like that." A lump came to her throat. Kneeling down, she threw her arms around the creature and kissed its pointy ears.

The dragon stopped sobbing. When Sophy drew back, she realized that her apron pocket felt very warm. She reached inside for the little bag of stones she'd almost forgotten about. When she lifted it out, she knew at once that something strange was happening.

Fingers trembling, she opened the bag and poured the rough, gray stones onto the ground.

One of them wasn't gray any longer. It had turned a deep, glowing amber—the exact same color as the dragon's eyes.

Sophy picked it up and watched the stone grow brighter in the palm of her hand. It became hotter, too—so hot she didn't think she could hold it anymore. Yet somehow she didn't want to let go. . . .

Crack! The stone broke into two pieces.

The orange glow faded until the two parts of

the stone were gray and ordinary again.

Except . . . Sophy looked closer. The stone was hollow. Inside each part was a tiny cave filled with purple crystals. She gazed at the two pieces of rock in turn, studying the little forest of crystals inside. They glittered in the sunlight like hidden treasure.

"It's really beautiful!" she said to herself.

"Pretty!" agreed the dragon.

Sophy's mouth dropped open. "What did you say?"

"It's pretty!" repeated the dragon, but then his eyes welled with tears again. "But my wing hurts." He tried to flap his crooked wing.

Sophy took a moment to get her breath back. "You're

talking!" she gasped. "That's amazing! I think this stone must be magic."

The creature blinked and forgot to cry. "Well, it is *very* shiny!"

Sophy smiled.

"Maybe you see magic all the time, but it's never happened to me before! I'm Sophy."

"So-fee!" said the dragon, trying out the name. Then he coughed, and a little flame shot out of his mouth. "My name's Cloudtwister, but everyone calls me Cloudy for short. I'm a storm dragon."

Chapter Three

✦ •✦

The Bad Knight

A storm dragon?" Suddenly Sophy realized why it had become so windy in the orchard. "Are you doing that?" She pointed to the swirling leaves.

Cloudy nodded, pleased. "I'm still learning, though. I can only make little breezes!"

"Oh, so you're a young dragon!" That explained why Cloudy was so small, Sophy realized. He was just a baby.

Cloudy pricked up his ears. "What's that noise?"

There were voices and the clanking of armor not far away. Sophy remembered the shouting she'd heard just before the dragon crash-landed. "I think someone must have seen you fall into the trees, and they're coming to look for you." She bit her lip. "Oh dear! I should tell you . . . not everyone likes dragons."

Cloudy's eyes widened in alarm, and a sharp gust of wind buffeted round them. "My wing hurts and I can't fly away. Help me, Sophy!"

The men's voices were getting closer. Sophy

tried to think quickly. "Don't worry! I'll find somewhere for you to hide until they've gone, but you have to stay really quiet. Can you do that?"

"Yes!" Cloudy's purple tail swished eagerly. "Very quiet!"

Sophy put the hollow stone in her pocket and scanned the orchard. Where could she hide him? There was nothing here except apple trees. "I'm going to pick you up. Are you ready?"

She took hold of Cloudy and held him tight. It was like carrying a squishy puppy with wings.

The dragon's feet dangled below her waist, and his breath felt warm on her cheek. She hoped he wouldn't cough or sneeze. If he did, she might end up with scorched hair, and that would be really hard to explain to Mrs. Ricker!

Sophy carried him back to the tree where she'd been picking apples and carefully climbed

the ladder. At the top
she pushed the leaves apart and
squeezed Cloudy onto a branch. The little dragon
perched in the crook where the branch joined
the tree trunk, completely hidden by leaves.

"There you go! Try not to make a sound," she
whispered. "I'll come back to get you when it's
safe."

Sophy climbed down and gathered up the rest
of the stones and the bag, which she'd left on
the ground. She put everything into her pocket,
taking one more look at the two pieces of stone
with their crystals before she hid them with the
others.

Heavy footsteps sounded, and three men
marched through the trees. Sir Fitzroy, dressed

in silver armor,
arrived first, with two
guards following behind.

Sophy stifled a gasp.
Why did it have to be
him? Everyone knew
that Sir Fitzroy hated
creatures with magic.
Cook had told her the
story: Long ago, when
the knight was a
boy, a unicorn had
injured him with
its horn,

and he had detested magical animals ever since. Sophy couldn't help thinking that an animal as lovely as a unicorn wouldn't have hurt anyone without a very good reason!

"You there!" snapped Sir Fitzroy, looking down his long nose. "What are you doing?"

"I'm just picking apples, sir," Sophy told him. "Cook wants them for a pie."

"Then why are you standing a long way from your apple basket and right next to a damaged tree?" said Sir Fitzroy. "Tell me everything you've seen or you'll be punished!"

Sophy swallowed. Sir Fitzroy was known as the meanest knight in Arramia, and the way he glared at people made her shiver. She mustn't be scared, she told herself. She'd promised Cloudy that she'd help him, and nothing was going to stop her from doing that.

"I didn't see anything at all," she said firmly. "I was over there picking apples, and I heard a noise. Then I came down the ladder and saw that this tree was broken."

Sir Fitzroy leaned forward, his eyebrows drawn low. "You mean to tell me that you were right here and you didn't see the beast that caused this destruction?" He turned away before she could answer. "Honestly, girl! You need to learn to keep your eyes open."

"Yes, sir." Sophy took a long time going to fetch her basket of apples. She wanted to find out what Sir Fitzroy was up to.

One of the guards spoke. "If it really was a dragon, sir, won't it have taken off by now?"

Sir Fitzroy turned red. "It *was* a dragon, you fool! I saw it in the sky, and no one's seen it fly away again, which means it's still here, somewhere on the castle grounds. It may have landed here on purpose to attack the queen."

Sophy's eyebrows flew upward. She didn't think Cloudy could attack a tomato!

"I always knew the old king was too soft on these creatures," the knight continued. "The beasts are a danger to the kingdom! Fortunately, the queen agrees with me. I shall find this dangerous animal before it can do any more harm, and lock it up forever!"

Sophy felt a chill run through her. She couldn't believe Sir Fitzroy could say such terrible things! One of the guards noticed her lingering, so she had to pretend to be busy picking up the apples that she'd deliberately knocked out of the basket.

"There are lots of places the dragon might be hiding, sir," a guard said. "There's the courtyard, the fountains, the statue garden, the vegetable plot, the maze—"

"Get on with it, then!" interrupted the knight. "Gather more men together and start hunting. I want that dragon found before sunset!"

A tiny rustle came from the tree where Cloudy was hiding, but Sophy didn't dare look up into the branches. Any glance might give the little dragon away. She needed to wait till there was no one around to fetch him down again. She hooked the apple basket over her arm and hurried out of the orchard, hoping the men wouldn't decide to search the trees.

Her heart sank as she thought of Sir Fitzroy's plan to lock up the baby dragon. Poor Cloudy would never fly again and never get home to his dragon family. She felt for the stones in her apron pocket and held them tightly. Cloudy was only a baby dragon, and he needed looking after. She would make sure he stayed safe and free!

Chapter Four

★ ⁘ ✦

Dragon Hunt

Sophy's thoughts were whirling as she hurried back into the castle. Maybe if she watched from a window upstairs, she'd be able to see when it was safe to rescue Cloudy. She hoped he wasn't too lonely by himself!

"You're running late, Sophy!" Mrs. Ricker pounced on her as soon as she reached the kitchen. "Leave that fruit for Cook. You must come with me at once. Her Majesty has ordered a thorough clean of her chambers." She handed Sophy a broom and duster.

Sophy had no choice but to follow Mrs. Ricker along the red-carpeted hallway that led past the banquet hall and up the grand staircase to the queen's chambers.

"Everything must be spotless," ordered the housekeeper.

As soon as she'd gone, Sophy started polishing and dusting. It wasn't her favorite chore (that was mixing the icing for Cook's delicious cakes), but she knew she could do it quickly. She finished dusting and swept the floor. Then she ran to the window, opened it, and leaned out to see what was happening in the orchard.

Sir Fitzroy was standing in the statue garden with his arms folded. Guards swarmed around the fountains and the vegetable plot, but the orchard was empty. Sophy's heart lifted. If she could get back outside, she might be able to fetch Cloudy down from the tree and sneak him out of the castle gates.

Picking up her broom and duster, Sophy rushed to the door and looked out. Drat! Mrs. Ricker was right outside in the corridor dusting the picture frames. How was she going to get to the orchard without the housekeeper giving her a new list of chores?

Desperate, she looked out the window again. A patch of trees swayed in the middle of the orchard. The wind was stirring their branches and fluttering their leaves. If Cloudy was making that happen, it might mean he was scared. She hoped the guards wouldn't notice that it was only windy in one part of the garden!

Sophy opened the window wider and looked at the thick ivy growing up the castle wall.

If she were brave, she could climb right down it without Mrs. Ricker seeing her. Was the ivy strong enough to hold her? She climbed onto the windowsill, swung her leg out, and tested the ivy's strength with her foot.

Yes, it seemed pretty sturdy.

She threw her broom and duster onto the grass. Then she climbed carefully down the ivy, choosing firm handholds and footholds all the way.

At the bottom she brushed the dirt off her

apron and hid the broom and duster behind a bush. Now all she had to do was fetch Cloudy.

She kept a lookout for Sir Fitzroy and the guards as she ran across to the trees.

The orchard was still empty, and Sophy breathed a sigh of relief when she reached the ladder.

"Cloudy, are you all right?" she whispered. There was no reply.

Maybe Cloudy couldn't understand her when the magical stone was hidden inside the little cloth bag. Delving into her apron pocket, she found the hollow rock with the beautiful crystals. Then she tried again.

"Cloudy, it's me! I'm coming up the ladder."

She climbed up and parted the branches, but the place where she'd left Cloudy was empty.

Panicking, she reached higher into the tree, pushing leaves away from her face. But there was no baby dragon there.

Heart thumping, Sophy climbed down and scanned the orchard. Where was he? Had Sir Fitzroy found him and thrown him in a cage? No, that couldn't be right. She could hear the guards calling to one another as they searched.

"Cloudy, where are you?" she hissed. "It's me—Sophy."

She ran up and down the rows of apple trees, looking up into the branches. There was no cute purple face peering down at her and no breeze stirring the leaves.

Sophy looked around wildly. Cloudy couldn't have just disappeared! The statue garden at one end of the orchard was full of guards. At the other end was the maze. She ran toward the maze, hoping that was the right guess.

Thick hedge walls closed around her. Sophy ran left and right, checking each corner to see if a little purple dragon was hiding there. The maze was enormous, and the twisty turns seemed to go on forever. At last she reached the center and ran straight into Tom, who was clipping the hedges.

"You're in a hurry." Tom put down his clippers and wiped his forehead. "What are you doing?"

"Nothing, really," said Sophy, scanning the place for Cloudy.

"Have you lost something?" asked Tom.

"Er, no, of course not." Sophy knew she didn't sound very convincing!

"You're looking for that creature that crashed into the orchard, aren't you?" said Tom. "They think it's a dragon. I thought about joining in the hunt too, but I reckon the silly monster flew off ages ago!"

"He's not a silly monster!" Sophy blurted out. "I mean . . . he could be a really nice little dragon. Maybe he's just a baby."

Tom folded his arms, his freckled face curious. "You've seen him! Did you tell Sir Fitzroy?"

Sophy's cheeks flushed. "No! And I'm not going to, either! He wants to put Cloudy in a cage, and that's a horrible thing to do."

Tom shook his head. "Sir Fitzroy is a power-ful man. You don't want to get on the wrong side of him!"

"I'm not scared of him!" Sophy said, although she was a little. She glanced at Tom. She found him a bit annoying sometimes, but he was always kind to animals. She'd seen him look after the horses in the royal stable. If he agreed to help, it would make finding Cloudy a whole lot easier. She took a deep breath. "I'm going to make sure Cloudy escapes. Do you want to help me?"

"Sure!" said Tom, grinning. "We can have our own dragon hunt. But why do you call him Cloudy? You say it as if you know it's his real name."

"Promise you won't tell?" said Sophy, and Tom

44

nodded. "I *do* know it's his real name because he told me so. Something amazing happened today: I discovered a magical stone, and now I can talk to a dragon!"

Chapter Five

✦ ⋆ ✦

A Trail of Cake Crumbs

Sophy and Tom agreed to search different parts of the castle grounds and meet back at the maze. Sophy wasn't sure Tom believed her about being able to talk to the dragon.

She didn't blame him, really. She could hardly believe it herself!

It was tricky searching the garden with so many guards around. Sophy had to dodge behind statues and rosebushes so they wouldn't see her. She searched hard, but there was still no sign of Cloudy.

"Did you find him?" she asked anxiously when she met Tom in the maze an hour later.

Tom shook his head. "I did see strange marks in the vegetable plot, though—almost like a dog's paw prints but with claw scrapes, too. I covered them over with earth before anyone else saw them."

"Those must be Cloudy's footprints!" said Sophy excitedly. "Did you see anything else?"

"Some of the beets had been pulled out of the

ground. It looked like they'd been eaten."

Sophy thought for a moment. "Maybe Cloudy got hungry. Which way did the footprints go?"

"They were all mixed up, so it was hard to tell."

"Let's start searching from there. Maybe we'll find another clue." Sophy dashed out of the maze toward the vegetable plot, but half-way across the garden she was stopped by a stern-looking Mrs. Ricker.

"Sophy, where were you?" The house-keeper frowned. "I've been calling you for ages."

"Oh! Um . . ." Sophy hoped Mrs. Ricker wasn't going to insist she explain what she'd been up to!

"There's a terrible mess in the kitchen,"

the housekeeper went on. "Cook left a window open. An animal must have climbed in and seen the chocolate cake that was meant for the queen's tea. I think it was probably a squirrel. Anyway, the cake is quite ruined! You must come and clean it up *at once.*"

Suspicion dawned in Sophy's mind.

"Yes, Mrs. Ricker. Of course." She cast a look at Tom before following the housekeeper into the kitchen.

Mrs. Ricker went away, muttering about asking Cook to bake something else. Sophy hurried to the kitchen table.

All the chocolate icing had been licked off the top of the cake, and there was a large hole in the middle, as if something had bitten right into it. Sophy felt even more suspicious.

"Cloudy?" she whispered softly. "Can you hear me?"

She thought she heard a rustling somewhere, but there was no sign of the dragon behind the cupboard or under the table. Then she noticed a trail of chocolate-brown cake crumbs leading across the floor. She followed them to the door of the pantry—the little room where Cook kept her bags of flour, jars of jam, and pots of spices.

Gently, Sophy opened the door and peered into the dark. "Cloudy?"

A snuffling sound came out of the gloom, followed by a sneeze. Sophy stepped back to avoid the burst of flame and the puff of smoke that followed. She wafted the smoke away with her hands and slipped into the pantry, closing the door behind her. "Cloudy, what's wrong?"

"Oh, Sophy!" sniffled Cloudy. "I've been a very bad dragon."

"You mean because you ate the chocolate cake?" Sophy searched around in the dark and found a tearstained Cloudy huddled next to a sack of porridge oats. She knelt down and put an arm round him. "Don't worry about that. You've had a terrible day—hurting your wing and every-thing. No wonder you were hungry!"

Cloudy hiccupped. "It's not just the cake! I was naughty to go flying by myself. My brother told me

I should wait till I was bigger, but I didn't listen."

A swirl of wind whisked around the pantry, rustling the bags of flour. Sophy patted Cloudy comfortingly, hoping to calm him down.

There was a quiet knock on the pantry door. "Sophy, it's me—Tom." The door opened, and Tom's face peered round. "Is the dragon here? Wow! Isn't he small!"

Sophy hugged Cloudy, who was trying to hide behind her. "Don't be scared. It's only my friend Tom. He won't hurt you."

Cloudy looked doubtfully at Tom and then crept over to sniff his shoes. "What is the freckled boy saying?"

"Can't you two understand each other?" Sophy handed Tom the hollow stone with the purple crystals inside. "Here! All the magic began when this stone broke into two pieces."

Tom looked at it curiously. "Hello, Cloudy, I'm Tom. Can you understand what I'm saying?"

Cloudy wrinkled his little face and looked confused. It was clear that he didn't understand at all. Sophy felt a fluttering inside. So the magical stone only worked for her. That was even more amazing!

"Are you trying to trick me?" Tom gave Sophy the stone back, frowning.

"No, I'm not—honestly!" she told him. Tom still looked doubtful.

Sophy turned to the little dragon. "Look, there isn't much time. Mrs. Ricker could come back any minute. Cloudy, I'm taking you somewhere safe until I've thought of a plan to get you out of the castle. Wait here a second."

Sophy dashed to the laundry room. She grabbed some of the sheets and clothes folded

neatly on the side and stuffed them higgledy-piggledy into a large wicker laundry basket.

Then she hurried back to the pantry.

Tom went out to check the corridor. "There's no one here," he called back. "I'll clean up the cake crumbs. Go quickly before someone sees you!"

"Thanks, Tom." Sophy put down the basket and lifted up the clothes. "Hop in, Cloudy. You'll be completely hidden in here."

Cloudy climbed in and curled up, and Sophy arranged the sheets and clothes over the top of him. "Just try not to make any flames," she added nervously.

"Yes, Sophy!" Cloudy's voice was muffled by the sheets.

Sophy checked that every bit of the dragon was covered. Then she picked up the basket. It felt much heavier, but she could carry it quite easily.

She left the kitchen and took the spiral staircase used by the servants. She met Mrs. Ricker at the top of the steps, and her heart sank.

"Oh, Sophy! I need to speak to you." Mrs. Ricker glanced at Sophy and then frowned at the laundry basket. "Keep out of the garden for a while. The guards are searching for some dreadful beast that's invaded the grounds. They're saying it could be a dragon."

"Yes, Mrs. Ricker." Sophy tried to edge past. She could feel Cloudy wriggling in the bottom of the basket. The sheets on top of him started to quiver.

The housekeeper put a hand on Sophy's arm. "Be very careful!" She lowered her voice. "This beast must have some deadly plan. The queen has given orders for it to be locked in the dungeon when it's found."

Sophy nodded, not trusting herself to speak.

As soon as she turned the corner, she began to run, the basket bumping against her knees. She reached her bedroom and dashed inside, shutting the door behind her. Then she put the basket down on her woolen rug and pulled the sheets off Cloudy.

The little dragon had fallen fast asleep.

Chapter Six

✦ ∴ ✦

Furry Friends

Sophy gazed at the little sleeping dragon. He looked so cute with his soft purple cheeks and a faint curl of smoke coming from his nostrils.

How could anyone think of throwing him into a dungeon? Now and then he gave a little squeaky snore and his wings twitched. Sophy wondered if he was dreaming about flying. His left wing was still crooked. How was she going to help him get back to his family when he couldn't fly?

Sophy took the bag of stones from her apron pocket. All the rocks were dull and gray except for the magical one. She tucked the bag with all the ordinary stones into the back of her sock drawer. Then she took out some cotton thread and tied the two halves of hollow rock together before fastening the thread around her neck. The rock looked as if it were whole again.

Sophy smiled. Wearing the magical stone as a necklace would be much better than picking it up every time she wanted to talk to Cloudy. The rock was tucked beneath her clothes, so there was no danger of anyone seeing it.

Cloudy stirred and blinked at her with large amber eyes.

Sophy knelt down next to his basket. "Cloudy, I've been thinking. Maybe I could take a look at your wing and see how bad it is? Helping you get home would be a lot easier if you could fly."

Cloudy yawned and sat up, stretching out his crooked wing. "Okay, Sophy," he said bravely.

Sophy studied the wing anxiously. "Does it hurt if you move it?"

Cloudy tried to flap the wing but hardly managed to lift it at all. His little face crumpled, and tears came to his eyes.

Sophy's heart ached to see him upset again. "Don't worry," she said. "Cook has a brown medicine that she gives me when I hurt myself. Maybe it works on dragons, too."

Cloudy sniffed miserably. "Mummy always gives me dragonweed."

"Dragonweed? Is that a plant?" Sophy wrinkled her forehead. She'd never heard of dragonweed, but Tom might know what it was since he did so much gardening.

Two big tears rolled down Cloudy's cheeks.

"I miss my mummy and I'm sooo hungry!" The last part almost turned into a howl, and a burst of wind whirled round the bedroom. Sophy had to shush him and stroke his ears. When Cloudy grew calmer, the wind dropped again.

"If I go to fetch you some food, do you promise you'll stay quiet?" she asked him.

Cloudy nodded eagerly. "The cake was yummy, but I need more to nibble."

"I'll find you something." Sophie smiled.

Dragons obviously had big appetites even when they were young!

She crept down to the kitchen to look for left-overs that no one would miss. While Cook was outside talking to the delivery boy, she took a piece of cherry pie, three carrots, and a bowl of macaroni and cheese. Her stomach rumbled, reminding her that she was pretty hungry too. Wrapping the food in her apron, she hurried away and nearly ran straight into Sir Fitzroy.

"Someone find me that dragon!" he yelled as he stormed down the corridor.

Sophy hung back in the shadows until he'd passed by. Then she dashed upstairs as fast as she could. She found Cloudy curled up in her bed but still awake. His purple tail looked funny sticking out the side of the quilt.

"Here you are." She set the food down carefully.

"I don't really know what dragons eat, so I hope you like it."

Cloudy leaped out of bed. "Mmm—yum!" he said, taking a bite of carrot.

Sophy took a carrot too and sat down next to him. There was a scratching at the door. She jumped, then realized it was probably only Spaghetti, the castle cat, who liked to sleep on her bed in the afternoons. She opened the door and the big ginger cat strolled in and got halfway across the room before noticing Cloudy. Spaghetti gave a startled meow and her fur stood on end. Then she sprang into the corner and took up guard there, her green eyes fixed on the dragon.

Cloudy waved his tail at the cat and went on eating. After munching the carrots, he scoffed the cherry pie in one bite and then peered doubtfully at the bowl of pasta. "What's that?"

"It's macaroni and cheese. You eat it with this." Sophy showed him a spoon. "Although now that I think about it, spoons are probably a bit tricky for a dragon."

Cloudy licked the pasta suspiciously and a huge smile spread over his face. "I *love* macaroni and sneeze!"

"Macaroni and *cheese*!" said Sophy, laughing. Cloudy dipped his face to the bowl, gobbled up the pasta, and licked his lips.

"*More* macaroni and sneeze, Sophy?" he purred.

"I don't think there *is* any more," said Sophy, amazed at how much food the little dragon ate.

There was a whistling from outside, and she ran to open the window. Tom was walking past, pushing a wheelbarrow.

"Tom!" she called softly.

He stopped underneath the window. "What's up? Is everything okay?"

"We're fine." She looked around, checking that no one was close enough to hear. "Do you know what dragonweed looks like?"

"Yes, it's a little plant with orange flowers. There's a lot of it in the fields outside the castle."

Sophy was going to ask more questions about the dragonweed, but a guard came round the corner. Tom gave her a wave and pushed his wheelbarrow away.

Closing the window, Sophy thought hard about what Tom had said and her plan for Cloudy's escape. She could sneak out, search for the dragonweed, and bring it back to fix Cloudy's wing. But what if she couldn't find the right plant? Then Cloudy would still be trapped.

No, she would take Cloudy with her. They would go while everyone was having dinner. There would still be guards at the gate, but she would get past them somehow. There had to be a way!

Turning back, she was surprised to find that Spaghetti had jumped onto the bed to join them. The dragon padded up to Sophy's pillow and breathed on it to make it warm. "There you go, kitty!"

Spaghetti curled up on the cozy pillow, looking very satisfied. Cloudy began singing softly. Sophy didn't catch all of it, but she heard a line about flying through moonlit clouds.

When the little dragon had finished singing, Sophy asked, "Where's your home, Cloudy? Do you live near here?"

Cloudy shook his head. "We live on the rocky cliffs by the Great Ocean. But we are always flying—to the Whispering Forest, where the star wolves sing, and over the grasslands, where the unicorns gallop. Sometimes we go to the Dusty Desert to see the firebirds soaring from the volcano. Sometimes we go to the tallest mountains to see the cloud bears making mist with their ice-cold breath."

Sophy imagined each place as he spoke about it—the whispering trees in the forest and mist floating over the mountains. "Wow! You've seen so much."

"That is our life," explained Cloudy. "We are storm dragons! We bring rain clouds from the ocean and blow them across the dry land. My brother says that's how the trees and flowers and vegetables get the water they need to grow."

"Then you're helping the whole kingdom!" cried Sophy. "It sounds amazing. I wish I could fly across the kingdom like that."

"I was meant to stay on my brother's back," said Cloudy, looking sad. "Not fly off by myself . . ."

Sophy hugged him tight. "Don't worry, Cloudy. When the sun goes down, I'll help you find a way out of here. You'll be back with the other dragons by morning."

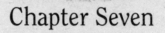

Chapter Seven

✦ ⦁ ✦

A Whirlwind in the Castle

Sophy's plan to sneak out at sunset was ruined when Mrs. Ricker asked her to serve Queen Viola and Sir Fitzroy their supper. She carried the plates and silver serving dishes back and forth, growing more nervous with every minute that passed.

Cook noticed that Sophy wasn't herself. When the queen and Sir Fitzroy were eating their dessert, she made the girl sit down and have a slice of the apple pie she'd baked to replace the ruined chocolate cake.

Cook studied her with kindly eyes. "What

have you been doing today that's made you look so tired?"

"Picking apples and cleaning the queen's chambers, as well as other things." Sophy smiled.

Cook was always nice to her. She felt bad that she couldn't explain about Cloudy. Cook sent her upstairs for a rest, and Sophy hurried away gratefully. She found the little dragon by her bedroom window, gazing at the sky.

"Time to go, Cloudy."

Sophy pulled off her maid's apron and put on the only other clothing she owned—a midnight-blue dress that she wore to go to the village on her day off. It had been mended in lots of places, but it was still a beautiful color. Wearing it would make her harder to spot in the darkness. Finally she took the bag of stones out of her sock drawer and put them in her dress pocket, just in case they came in handy.

She lifted Cloudy into the laundry basket again, covered him up with clothes and sheets, and slipped into the corridor. She got halfway down the back stairs when she heard Mrs. Ricker arguing with Cook at the bottom.

"You're too soft on that girl!" snapped the housekeeper. "I bet she's up to mischief."

"Sophy has a good head on her shoulders," Cook replied. "And a kinder heart than a lot of people in this castle. All this nonsense about a fierce dragon on the loose! I bet the poor creature means no harm to anyone."

Sophy smiled. At least Cook wasn't against dragons like Sir Fitzroy. She swung round with the basket and hurried back up the stairs.

"We'll have to go the other way," she whispered

to Cloudy. "We definitely can't risk Mrs. Ricker seeing you."

She didn't dare climb down the ivy in the dark, and she didn't think Cloudy would manage it either. So the only other way out was the grand staircase.

"Where are we going, Sophy?" piped up Cloudy from under the sheets.

"Shh! We'll be out soon." Sophy crept along the thick red carpet and down the wide staircase with its golden handrails. She could get into big trouble for this. She wasn't supposed to bring washing baskets down the grand staircase at all, let alone one with a dragon inside!

Voices were drifting through the big, arched doorway that led into the grand banquet hall. Queen Viola and Sir Fitzroy must still be in there, eating apple pie and drinking coffee.

"So I've put twice as many guards on the gate and along the walls," said Sir Fitzroy. "I believe that the nasty little beast is still somewhere in the castle grounds. But we'll find him, and then he'll be sorry!"

"Thank goodness I have you defending the castle, Sir Fitzroy," said the queen. "I've never liked magical animals. How can you trust a creature that breathes fire or sings to the stars?"

Sophy's cheeks reddened. She was glad that Cloudy didn't understand what Queen Viola had just said. How could she think such things? Cloudy was so sweet and lovely, and his storm magic was amazing!

Sophy reached the bottom of the stairs and held her breath as she tiptoed past the huge doorway to the banquet hall. She could see

Queen Viola at the table wearing her gold crown. Sir Fitzroy sat opposite, clothed in a black velvet robe instead of his usual armor.

Sophy walked faster, but the edge of the washing basket knocked against a silver vase on a table. The empty vase toppled over with a loud clang. Her heart sank. She hoped no one had heard it.

"You there!" yelled Sir Fitzroy. "I want to talk to you!"

Sophy froze. Both Sir Fitzroy and Queen Viola were looking her way. She glanced down, but Cloudy was still hidden beneath the layers of sheets and clothes.

"Yes, sir," she called back, trying to sound normal. "Shall I ask Cook to send in more coffee?"

"No, I don't want coffee!" Sir Fitzroy's fierce eyes seemed to see right through her. "You're the one who was in the orchard when the beast landed, aren't you? I want to ask you some more questions. Come here at once, girl."

Sophy's heart pounded. If she put the basket down, Cloudy might get the wrong idea and jump out. Going closer with the basket might be even worse. If Cloudy were seen here, he'd be captured in seconds.

"Sorry, sir, but I have an important errand," she said cheerfully. "I'll finish up and be back in a few minutes—"

"GET OVER HERE AT ONCE!" Sir Fitzroy banged his fist on the table, making the dishes shake. "You can't tell me you'll come back later. You're nothing but a serving maid!"

Sophy's hands tightened on the edge of the basket. She longed to tell Sir Fitzroy that there was no need to be rude. When the old king was alive, no one would have been allowed to yell like that.

The clothes at the top of the basket shook, and two aprons and a pillowcase blew into the air. A gust of wind swirled round Sophy.

Then a sheet floated out of the basket, followed by a pair of the queen's royal bloomers, trimmed with golden thread. Sophy made a grab for them, but they flew through the arched doorway into the banquet hall, chased by the gathering wind.

More clothes and sheets sailed into the hall as the wind became wilder. Stormy gusts whipped past Sophy, heading straight for the queen and her favorite knight.

The queen gasped and clutched her crown. "What's happening?" she cried. "Is this some kind of spell?"

"I will defend you, Your Majesty!" Sir Fitzroy

drew his sword, only to have it knocked from his hand by the wind.

Sophy's eyes widened. Five small whirlwinds were snaking across the hall, twisting and turning as if they were dancing. The silverware rattled on the banquet table, and the royal tablecloth flew upward, scattering pie crumbs everywhere.

The queen caught sight of her underwear sailing up to the ceiling and shrieked, "Do something, Sir Fitzroy!"

Sir Fitzroy didn't reply. His black robe had blown right over his head, and he was too busy trying to fight his way out of it.

"Cloudy, are you making it windy on purpose this time?" whispered Sophy.

Cloudy popped up from beneath the last sheet in the basket. "Yes, I am!" He beamed. "The nasty man shouldn't shout at you like that."

Sophy's throat tightened. No one had ever stood up for her like this before!

The five whirlwinds twirled on, rattling the royal pictures in their frames and making chairs slide across the floor. Now all the laundry was caught up in the twisters, spinning and dancing all over the place, leaving Cloudy completely uncovered.

Sophy put down the basket and grabbed the little dragon. Sir Fitzroy was still tangled up in his robe and the queen was trying to catch her royal underwear. This was their chance!

"You're amazing," Sophy told the dragon. "But we have to get you out of here!"

Sophy ran down the corridor and bolted through the front door into the night. Darkness closed around her as she held Cloudy tight. Her heart was racing. They'd almost made it! Now she just had to get over the drawbridge and past the gatehouse.

She dashed down the castle steps and ran to the drawbridge, but stopped short when she came to a locked gate. She peered through the gloom, feeling puzzled. Why had they locked the gate that led to the drawbridge? She couldn't even see the wooden bridge on the other side. There was nothing but empty blackness.

A feeling of horror swept over her. The

drawbridge wasn't there. Sir Fitzroy must have ordered the guards to pull it up. And the drawbridge was the only way across the moat.

She and Cloudy were trapped.

Chapter Eight

✦ .•✱

Dragonweed

Why are we stopping, Sophy?" asked Cloudy.

Sophy stared at the emptiness where the draw-

bridge should have been. A cold feeling of dread

grew inside her. She didn't want to panic—that would only upset Cloudy—but what was she going to do?

"I just need to think," she told the little dragon. "The guards have pulled up the drawbridge, and I don't know any other way across the moat."

"What is a moat?" Cloudy jumped down from her arms and sniffed the gate in front of them.

"It's the big circle of water that stretches around the castle wall," explained Sophy.

Cloudy climbed onto the wall to take a look.

Sophy climbed up beside him. Beneath them the moat glinted in the faint moonlight. She wished there were a way to get down; then maybe they could swim across together. She'd swum in the moat once with Tom, although they'd climbed in from the other side.

"Cloudy, can you swim?"

"Yes, but I don't like it very much," Cloudy said anxiously.

Behind them the castle door burst open. A troop of guards holding lanterns marched down the steps, while Sir Fitzroy stood at the top, glaring round. "Search the whole grounds!" he shouted. "That beast is out here somewhere, and its magic is already ruining our castle. Don't come back without it!"

Sophy's heart thumped. The guards could find them in seconds. Cloudy would be captured, and she would be in deep trouble. She was a maid—she was supposed to clean and dust, not rescue magical animals and set them free!

She glanced down at the moat again. It wasn't as big a drop as she'd thought. It was their only way out—if they were brave enough to take it.

"Cloudy," she whispered. "I think we have to jump in the moat. They'll catch us otherwise."

"No moat!" whimpered Cloudy. "Swimming is yucky. I want my wings to work. I want to fly!" He tried to hide his face against Sophy's shoulder.

"We'll jump together," said Sophy. "Please, Cloudy."

The baby dragon shivered and shook his head.

"I'll hold on to you. I promise," Sophy pleaded.

At last Cloudy nodded.

Sophy tried to breathe slowly to calm her nerves. She could do this. The moat was safe, and she knew how to swim. Standing on top of the wall, she held Cloudy tight. Then she jumped off.

For a few moments they fell through the darkness. Then they hit the moat with a splash. The water closed over their heads before they floated back to the surface. Sophy took a big gulp of air and looked around. She realized she'd let go of Cloudy when they hit the water. Where was he?

The little dragon's face popped up beside her. "Cloudy! Are you all right?" Sophy gasped.

Cloudy flapped his one good wing to keep

himself afloat, splashing her with water. "Yes. But yuck—this is horrible!"

"You're very brave!" said Sophy. "Quick, let's get to the bank."

Together they swam to the other side and pulled themselves onto the grassy bank. They lay there for a minute, dripping and trying to catch their breath. Sophy's blue dress was soaked, and she had to empty the water out of her shoes. Cloudy shook himself, showering her with water all over again. He sneezed, and a little flame shot out of his nostrils.

A lantern appeared at the top of the wall, and a guard called, "I think I saw something."

"Shall we check down there?" another guard replied. "It must have been something big— those splashes were huge."

"Quick!" Sophy scrambled up and dodged behind the nearest tree.

Cloudy rushed after her and clung on to her leg. "I'm scared!"

"Don't worry!" Sophy picked him up. "Tom told me where the dragonweed grows. I'm going to find some for you. I'm hoping it'll fix your wing."

A colossal creaking followed by a booming sound made them both jump. Sophy knew it was the drawbridge being lowered, and that meant guards would be coming down the hill to search for Cloudy.

Keeping to the shadows, she rushed away from the moat and climbed the fence into the field next door. Setting Cloudy down, she scoured the grass.

"Dragonweed has orange flowers," she muttered to herself. "Where is it?"

The moon came out from behind a cloud,

casting its pale light over the meadow.

Sophy was glad for the extra light until she remembered that the guards would be able to find them more easily. She crouched down, searching desperately. There were pink trillies and white star-candy flowers, but nothing that looked orange.

Suddenly Sophy spotted some flame-colored petals dotted among the grass. The plant had pale-green leaves, and the orange flower was shaped like a bell.

"Cloudy, is this dragonweed?" she hissed.

Cloudy bounded over. "Yes! Well done, Sophy."

"How does it work? Do you have to eat it?" She picked the flame-colored flower and offered it to him.

He shook his head. "Not the flowers—the leaves."

"Oh!" Sophy swiftly picked the dragonweed leaves and gave them to Cloudy.

He chewed them eagerly before lifting his crooked wing. "It's starting to work." He gave a huge belch, and a green flame shot out of his mouth. "More, more!"

Sophy picked more dragonweed leaves.

Cloudy munched those too and then flapped his wings. This time his injured left wing looked as strong as the right one!

A row of bobbing lantern lights came down the hill toward them.

"Go on, Cloudy! Fly!" shouted Sophy. The little dragon started beating his wings.

Sophy ran alongside him, flapping her arms and willing him to fly. His wingbeats grew stronger and stronger, and his feet lifted from the ground. He turned his amber eyes to Sophy, a smile spreading over his puppylike face.

"I love you, Sophy! I'll miss you!" He soared into the air.

Sophy watched him rise higher and higher.

Then she dodged behind some bushes as guards rushed into the meadow.

"Did you hear that strange squeaking?" one guard said. "Do you think that was the dragon?"

"Must have been," said another. "Look at that!"

Sophy peeped through the leaves to see what the guard meant. The moon had come

out from behind a cloud again, flooding the sky with pale light. A dark shape was moving closer. At first it seemed like another cloud, but as it grew, Sophy saw that it was a huge flight of dragons! Their wings were rising and falling in time with one another.

A shout went up from the guards. "Arm the battlements!"

The wind grew stronger and the trees swayed. The dragons swooped down until they reached a small, winged shape that was flying up to meet them. Cloudy had found his dragon family at last!

The flight of dragons whirled around and flew away into the distance, taking their baby dragon with them.

Chapter Nine

✦ ⁂ ✦

The Magic in the Stone

Sophy waited till the guards had gone back up the hill. Then she came out of her hiding place. She searched the dark sky for Cloudy and the other dragons, but she was sure they must be far away by now.

Suddenly she felt really tired, and her eyes ached. She missed Cloudy. There were so many things she wished she'd asked him. Were there many storm dragons in Arramia? What did the Great Ocean sound like? What did it feel like to fly?

Brushing leaves off her damp dress, she hurried up the hill and across the drawbridge. Sir Fitzroy was standing by the front door to the castle yelling at the guards. Then he stormed inside and slammed the castle door.

Sophy was turning away when she noticed a dark, cloudlike shape moving toward the castle very quickly. She caught her breath. It wasn't a cloud. It was a dragon . . . and it was much too big to be Cloudy! She rushed to the castle wall.

A huge creature with dark-green scales

swooped down and hovered beside the castle wall. The dragon looked just like Cloudy, with the same amber-colored eyes.

"I'm Windrunner—Cloudy's brother," growled the dragon softly. "And you must be Sophy."

Sophy's voice stuck in her throat. "P-pleased to meet you!"

Windrunner blinked slowly. "It's pretty strange, talking to a human. I didn't believe Cloudy when he first told us."

"Hello, Sophy!" Cloudy peered down from his

brother's back.

Sophy grinned. "Cloudy!
I didn't see you up there."

"I told the other dragons all about you!" Cloudy
beamed. "Then I made Windrunner fly back in

case that terrible man
was being mean to you
again!"

"Don't worry—I'm
fine!" said Sophy.

"Why don't you come with us
for a ride?" said Windrunner. "I
know the other storm dragons
really want to meet you."

"I'd love to!" Sophy felt
a fluttering in her stomach.
She couldn't believe she was going to
fly on a dragon. "It's really kind of you!"
she told Windrunner.

"Any friend of Cloudy's is a friend of
mine." Windrunner flew closer to the castle
wall. "Hop on!"

Sophy scrambled onto Windrunner's scaly back and sat down behind Cloudy.

The baby dragon grinned at her. "You're going to love flying!"

Sophy hugged Cloudy tight as Windrunner soared into the air. A tingle ran down her back as they gained speed, and her hair streamed out behind her in the wind. She gazed down at the lantern-lit castle, amazed at how small everything looked from high above.

With a few more beats of Windrunner's huge wings, they left the castle far behind. After a while Cloudy fell asleep, and Sophy watched the land roll by beneath them.

It was still dark, but when the moon came out from behind the clouds she could see houses, fields, and woods. Windrunner climbed high, and wisps of cloud clung to Sophy's dress and

hair. She was sure she heard music in the distance and wondered if it was the song of the star wolves. She strained to listen, but it vanished beneath the breeze.

As dawn drew closer, the sky lightened and the two planets shone in the morning light. Sophy's heart began to race. There were no houses and villages on the ground beneath them. This must be the wilds—the place where the magical creatures lived. There were strange sights everywhere. Sophy stared at the giant red-and-white toadstools growing in a forest clearing and smiled at a cloud of glittering butterflies dancing in a meadow.

Windrunner flew above a winding river that gleamed like a silver ribbon in the morning light. At last his wings grew slower, and he glided down to an island in the middle of the river. Wingbeats filled the air as the other storm dragons flew down to meet them. Thunder roared and wind blasted Sophy's face so that she had to close her eyes. She heard voices on the breeze, and she knew the storm dragons were calling to one another.

Windrunner landed smoothly, and Sophy slid off his back onto the grass. Cloudy woke up and flapped down beside her.

Dragons gathered round them, looking curiously at Sophy. With long tails and round snouts, they looked like Cloudy and Windrunner, but much, much bigger.

"Greetings, child." A dragon with a serious face and a long, bumpy tail stepped forward. "My name is Mistral. Do you understand what I'm saying?"

"Yes!" Sophy tried not to feel nervous with all the dragons looking at her. "I have a magic stone—"

"Show us this stone, child," said Mistral, his eyes brightening.

Sophy lifted the thread over her
neck and pulled the pieces
of the stone apart to show
them the cave of purple crystals
that lay inside.

A rumble like thunder passed
round the circle of dragons.

"That is a Speaking Stone,"
said Mistral. "I haven't seen
one in a very long time. You
must be careful with it,
child. A Speaking Stone is
very powerful and very
precious. Each stone
chooses a keeper and
will work for that person alone."

"Oh! So that's why it wouldn't
work for Tom." Sophy took out the little

bag and showed them the other rocks inside. "So these other stones I found could be magical too? Do they all let people talk to dragons?"

"Yes, but not just dragons," Mistral told her. "The Speaking Stones let you talk to any magical creature."

Sophy's eyes lit up. "That's amazing! But are you sure I should keep it? I'm a maid at the castle. I'm not anyone special."

"The stone chose you because you *are* special," Mistral said quietly. "We magical creatures need more help than ever now that the old king is gone. Some people are kind to us, but many more believe we're dangerous. There are dark times ahead."

Sophy met his gaze. "I'll do anything I can to help you."

"Thank you!" said Mistral, and all the dragons

bowed their heads to her. "Windrunner will fly you back to your castle now, and if you ever need us to carry you again, we would be honored to do so."

"Thank you!" Sophy climbed onto Windrunner's back and waved to the storm dragons. "Good-bye!" She smiled at Cloudy and gave him a special wave as Windrunner lifted off the ground.

While they flew high above the river, Sophy gazed at her Speaking Stone. Then she patted the bag of stones in her pocket. It was amazing to think that all those little rocks were magical too! Excitement fizzed inside her. The power in her stone would let her speak to all magical creatures. She'd be able to talk to a cloud bear or a firebird or a unicorn!

As they swooped over a green valley, three

golden songbirds flew up to meet them.

"Windrunner, you're carrying a girl on your back," said one of the birds in a voice like a tinkling bell.

"Yes, this is Sophy. She is our friend. She has a magical stone that lets her speak to us." Windrunner slowed and hovered in the air. "Sophy, meet the songbirds. They carry messages across the kingdom."

"Hello!" Sophy smiled at the birds, remembering the songbird that had helped her find the bag of stones.

"Do you have any news?" Windrunner asked the birds.

"Terrible news!" The songbirds beat their wings anxiously. "Danger is coming to the

magical animals of Misty Lake. A bad man is on his way there, and he has anger in his heart."

"What is he going to do?" Windrunner asked, but the songbirds had bobbed their heads and fluttered away.

"This is awful!" cried Sophy. "We should go to the lake right now."

"Are you sure?" said Windrunner. "Mistral said I should take you back to the castle. You'd be much safer there."

"I promised I would help you all, and I will!" Sophy declared.

"Then hold on tight!" Windrunner let out a puff of smoke and wheeled round, flying off at high speed.

Sophy held on as the trees and fields flashed by. After a few minutes she asked, "Which magical animals live by Misty Lake, Windrunner?"

"Sky unicorns and many other creatures too," the dragon told her.

Sky unicorns! A tingle ran down Sophy's back. She'd always hoped to meet magical animals, but now it was really happening!

At last a patch of silver appeared in the distance.

"There it is—Misty Lake!" Windrunner nodded his head toward the shimmering water.

Then he swooped lower, catching the breeze with his wings.

They flew over a herd of snow-white unicorns with golden horns and bright tails. Sophy gazed down at them in delight. She couldn't wait to meet them and have the next adventure begin!